FAREWELL TANA

WRITTEN BY ENRICA SOW
ILLUSTRATED BY J.S. ADAM

This book is dedicated to our Tana and Nana. Let us not forget all of the grandmothers in the world summoned by their many aliases, in various tongues. Your impact on our children is invaluable. We love you and treasure you!

...and enter My Paradise♥♥
وادخلي جنّتي...

The room was void of steaming pot smells. The roar of play silenced. This was very odd for a Saturday afternoon. It was unlike any other Saturday the boys knew or wanted to know. News of their grandmother's death arrived early that morning from Mauritania.

Gogo Halima let herself into the house. What she saw brought tears to her eyes. The boys were wrapped in an embrace with their mom. They leaned into one another trying to become one. At that moment, she was reassured that the contents inside her bag would help her nephews grieve.

A steady stream of mourners came to their house or called on the phone. They gathered to pray and offer their condolences. Just as quickly as they came, they left. If it weren't for Gogo Halima and her bag, the boys may have slipped into a summer long depression. She weaved through the crowd offering salaams with warm handshakes.

When she reached the hugging trio, she gave salaams, and began praying. Winking at her sister, she pried the boys loose and guided them to their bedroom.

"I brought something for the two of you." Gogo Halima whispered.

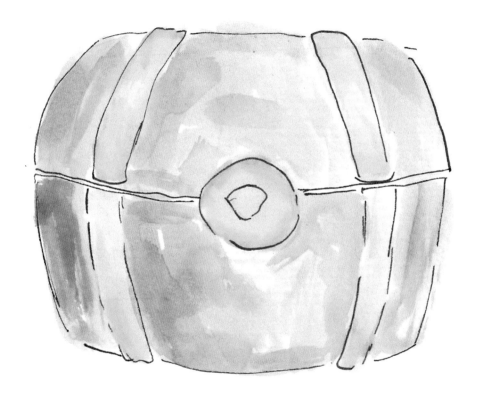

The boys perked up. Gifts from Gogo Halima were always interesting. From her reusable bag she pulled out a treasure chest. It looked just like those found in pirate stories.

"Wow! What's inside, GOLD?" asked Saleh.

"No, but you are going to fill it with a treasure more valuable than gold," she assured him.

"How? With what?" they pleaded.

"Well," she began "you understand that Tana will not be coming to visit this summer or any other summer."

The boys dropped their heads. She lifted their chins and continued.

"You are going to fill this treasure chest with Tana treasures. I want you to look around and find something that reminds you of a happy time with her. It can be a photo or something she gave you. When you find it, bring it to me," she instructed.

They sat and looked around for any sign of Tana. Suddenly, Saleh jumped up and ran to his drawer. He pulled out a smooth black rock that was as big as his hand. He gave it to Gogo Halima.

She asked, "How does this remind you of Tana?"

"Hassan, do you remember when we went to the river and saw the boat that drove out of the water and it turned into a bus?" Saleh asked excitedly.

"Oh yeah!" Hassan shrieked as he slapped his knee and began to laugh.

"Tana was so amazed. She laughed the whole time we were at the river, all the way home, and the next 100 days after that," continued Hassan.

"Yep! We were looking for rocks to use for wudu. She started telling stories about when she was a child and had to go to the river to wash clothes. In the middle of her story, her mouth dropped open and her eyes stared at the water. We followed her stare. That's when we saw a boat filled with tourists drive out of the water and up the ramp to the street. Water gushed out of its bottom and flowed back into the river."

"La ilaha illallah, if I tell this story back home they are going to call me a liar," Tana screamed with laughter.

As Gogo Halima dropped the black stone into the treasure box, Hassan came over with a picture. It was a picture of a Tana standing in the middle of a snow covered yard. She was wrapped in a leopard print shawl.

"I remember this picture. When she came back into the house, she immediately went to her bed and buried herself under the covers until dinner time. She was so cold!" Hassan recalled.

"I remember that year! She came for a visit during the winter instead of the summer. Your mom had to bring closed shoes to the airport because she knew that Tana would have on sandals," added Gogo Halima.

The boys added a bit of this and a bit of that. The more they added, the more they remembered, and the better they felt. They soon realized that they had a lot of memories to hold onto.

The door creaked open and their mom peeked in.

"What's all of the commotion? Are you having a party without me?" she inquired.

"Come in mom! Look at our Tana treasures!" they both yelled.

They told her all about the contents of the treasure chest. In between guests, they spent the rest of the afternoon laughing, sharing stories, and adding to the treasure chest. From that day forth, they brought out the treasure chest every time they wanted to feel close to Tana.

Made in the USA
Middletown, DE
22 July 2021